Activities created by Rotem Moscovich, Kate O'Sullivan, Monica Perez, Cynthia Platt,
Afsoon Razavi, Joyce White, Mark London Williams, Erica Zappy, and Emily Meyer.

ISBN: 978-0-547-23896-8

Design by Sara Gillingham
Special thanks to artists Rudy Obrero and Kaci Obrero
Manufactured in China
LEO 10 9 8 7 6 5
4500836980

Visit the following websites for games, activities, party kits, book lists and more:

www.pbskids.org/curiousgeorge
www.curiousgeorge.com

MISSING TOYS

George is looking for some special toys, but there are
too many things in his closet. The toys keep falling
out! Can you help George find the items pictured?

CIRCUS SIGHTS

What did George see at the circus?
Have fun drawing or use your stickers!

PARK PLAYTIME

There are so many things to see and do at the park with George.

How many bunnies do you see?

How many flowers do you see?

How many trees do you see?

WHICH WAY?

Which path should George take to find his way home?

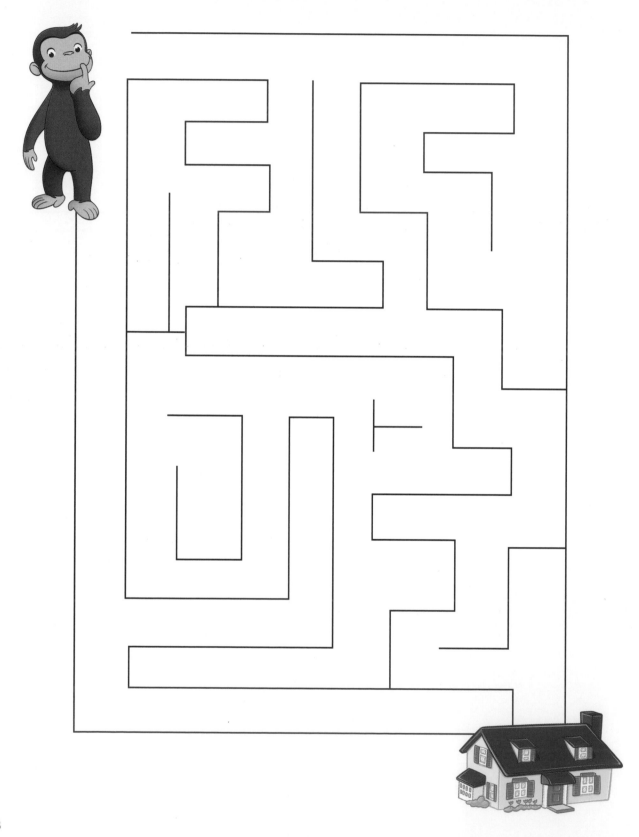

GONE FISHING

George has gone fishing. Draw in what you think he might catch.

FOLLOW THE LEADER

George is playing follow the leader! Help complete this picture of George and his dog friends with the puzzle stickers on page 65.

TIC-TAC-TOE

George loves to play tic-tac-toe! Grab a friend, decide who will be X's and who will be O's, and then mark your letter one space at a time. First one to get three across wins!

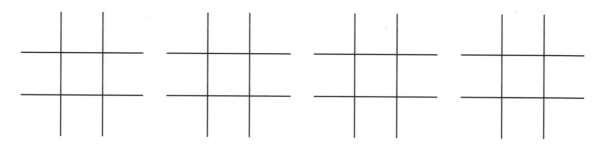

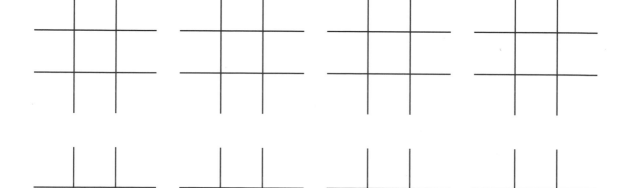

A VALENTINE FOR . . .

Using markers, crayons, and stickers on page 71, help Curious George make a valentine for the man with the yellow hat!

A TREE FOR GEORGE

Oh, my! George is trying to make a tree out of things he found around the house. Can you spot some of the objects he used and some that he didn't?

WATER WORLD

With his floaties and flippers,
George can swim like a fish.
Can you draw the perfect
place for him to take a dip?

CAMPING GEAR

Curious George and his friend are going camping! Can you find some of the items that they'll need . . . and maybe some they won't?

COUNT THE ANIMALS

Is it hard to count George's friends below one by one? Try circling different animal groups and then adding the groups!

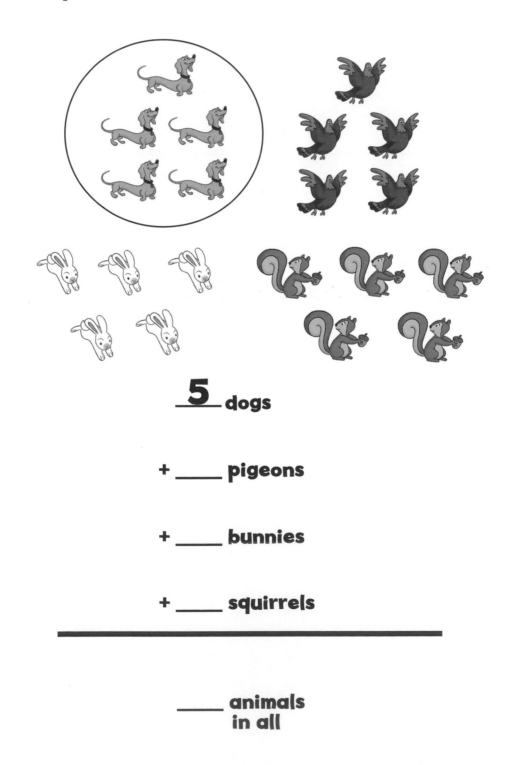

___5___ dogs

+ _____ pigeons

+ _____ bunnies

+ _____ squirrels

_____

_____ animals
in all

GEORGE'S GARDEN

George is watering his garden. Using markers, crayons, and stickers from pages 69 and 70, fill in what might be in George's garden.

WHAT'S UNDERNEATH?

George loves unwrapping presents to find out what's inside. But presents aren't the only things that can be unwrapped. Can you match the items below to their wrappings?

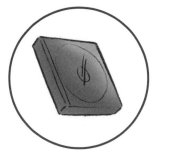

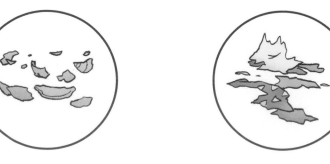

WINTRY WEATHER

Brrr! It's cold outside. Circle the images below that George wouldn't need on a cold, frosty day.

DONUT DELIVERY

George ordered too many donuts, and now he doesn't know what to do with them! Use the stickers on page 66 to complete the picture and see where George has hidden them all.

X MARKS THE SPOT

Follow these simple steps to create a treasure map on the next page—and then see if someone can find your hidden treasure!

To Make a Treasure Map

You will need these things:

* Markers or crayons
* A treasure!

1. Pick a secret spot in your backyard and hide something — that's the treasure.

2. On the next page, draw the outline of your backyard and then draw the important things that are in it. Here are some examples of landmarks: a swing set, trees, a swimming pool, a garden, a patio, or a shed.

3. Mark the spot where you've hidden the treasure with an "X" on your map. Show the map to your friends or family. See who can find the treasure first!

BUILD YOUR OWN RAFT

You'll need these things:

- Wooden craft sticks
- Pennies
- Glue

1. Line up several sticks vertically on a flat surface.

2. Take one stick and put glue along one side of it. Now place it horizontally across the sticks you lined up, about a quarter inch from their tops.

3. Take another stick with glue along one side and place it across the line of sticks, about a quarter inch from their bottom ends.

4. Let the sticks dry for an hour before putting the raft in water.

Check with an adult before floating your raft in the sink, bathtub, or kiddie pool. Guess how many pennies you can place on the raft before it sinks. Now test your theory by adding them one at a time.

A VISIT TO THE ZOO

What animals did George see at the zoo?

TIME TO EAT

George loves to go to Chef Pisghetti's restaurant.
But where is he? Can you find these items, too?

A TASTY TREAT

Happy birthday, George! What does his cake look like?

GOLFING WITH GEORGE

George would love to hit a hole in one.
Can you help him?

FURRY FRIENDS

Use the puzzle stickers on page 67 to complete
the picture of George and his friends!

HALLOWEEN HAUNTING

Using the stickers on page 72, can you help George
make this pumpkin into a jack-o-lantern?

CAN YOU COUNT BY TWO?

Counting by twos is often faster than counting each item if you have a lot of things to count. Match the socks below by drawing a line between each pair, and then count the pairs.

DOG DAZE

There are so many dogs with their owners—
but where is George? Can you find these things, too?

PAINTING FUN

What is George painting?
Help him create a masterpiece!

SAIL AWAY

Curious George is helping Bill sail his model sailboat.
Can you help George spot the other fun items?

WHAT'S GEORGE UP TO?

Are you a good predictor? In the pictures below, can you guess what happens next? Draw a line connecting the related images.

SHIPS AHOY!

Make a paper boat . . . and see if it can float.

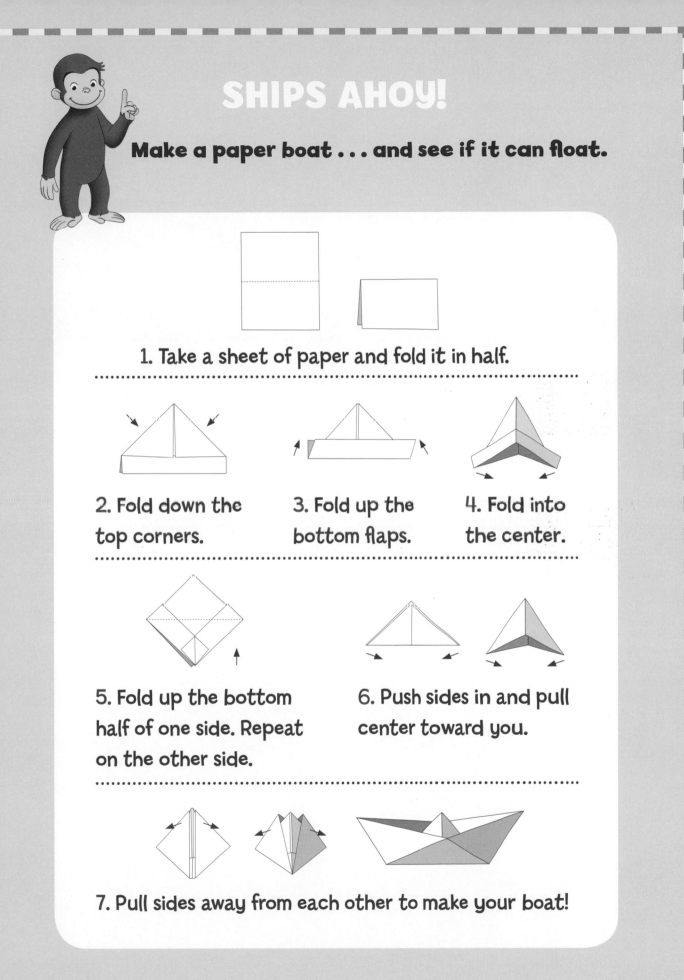

1. Take a sheet of paper and fold it in half.

2. Fold down the top corners.

3. Fold up the bottom flaps.

4. Fold into the center.

5. Fold up the bottom half of one side. Repeat on the other side.

6. Push sides in and pull center toward you.

7. Pull sides away from each other to make your boat!

PANDA'S PLAYTIME

George is having so much fun playing with the baby panda at the zoo. Use the stickers on page 68 to complete the picture of George and his new friend.

LET IT SNOW!

George needs some help making his snowman!
Use the stickers on page 72 to help him finish.

ANIMAL NOISES

Can you match the animal to the sound it makes?

WOOF!

BZZZ!

CLUCK!

MEOW!

BEAUTIFUL BUTTERFLIES

George loves butterflies! Use your finger to trace the lines below to find out which path will lead George to his butterfly friends.

You can make a butterfly of your very own. Take some tracing paper and copy the butterfly image below onto it. Color it darkly with crayons (be careful not to tear the paper!) and cut it out. Now tape it to your window for a beautiful stained-glass butterfly!

SPEED SKATING

George is taking his new roller skates out for a try, all four of them! Can you spot some of the things he sees as he whizzes by?

TOY TIME

George loves to play with his toys! Draw or use stickers from pages 77 and 78 to create a fun play area for him.

UP, UP, AND AWAY!

George likes to fly. Don't you? Here is how you can make a paper airplane of your own.

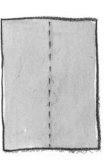

1. Fold a piece of paper in half the tall way, then unfold it again.

2. Fold down the top corners as shown in the picture.

3. Fold the edges in toward the crease you made in the middle.

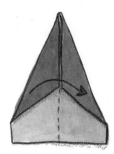

4. Now fold the plane in half and turn it to the side.

5. Make a wing from the front of the plane all the way to the back as shown in the picture.

6. You have a paper airplane!

HOW MANY HATS?

Large numbers are made up of smaller combinations of numbers. For example, two plus two is four, but three plus one is also four. Color hats in each row, count them, and fill in the blanks to get the same answer—six colorful hats!

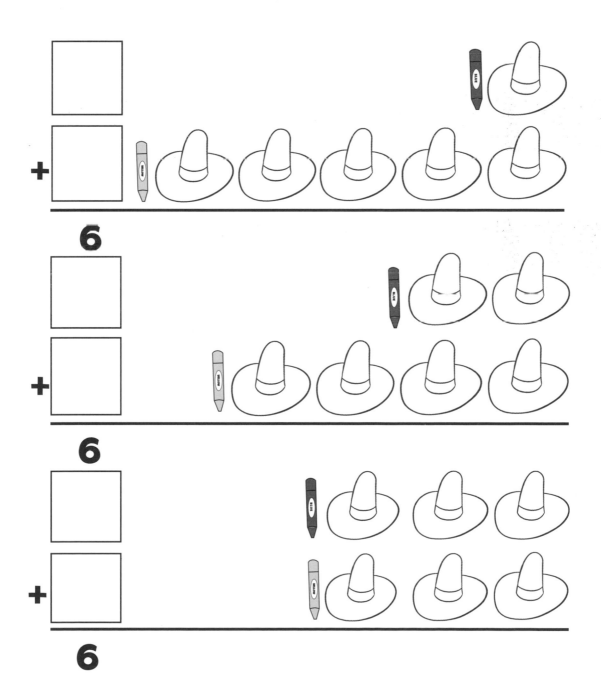

MUSEUM MONKEY

George is at the museum looking for a picture of one of his favorite animals—a monkey! Can you help him find it and the other items shown?

GEORGE'S SEASONS

George loves all four seasons. Can you draw or use stickers from pages 73, 74, 75, and 76 to show what he loves about each of the seasons?

FALL

WINTER

SPRING

SUMMER

GOOD NIGHT, GEORGE!

George is sleeping peacefully.
What do you think he's dreaming about?

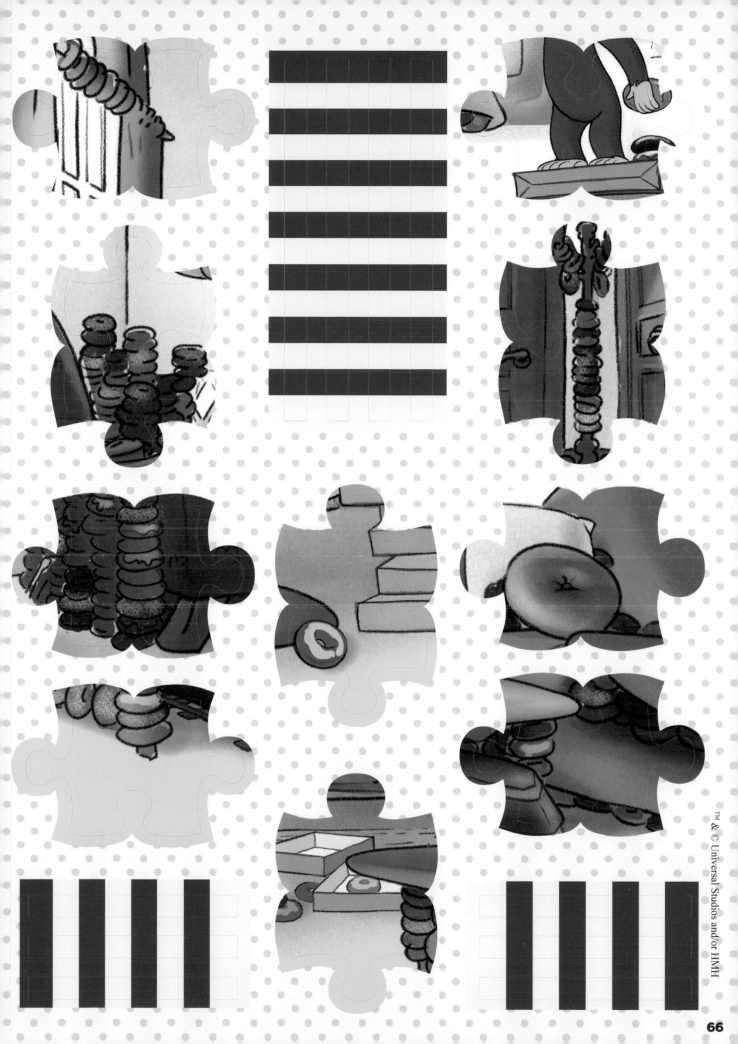

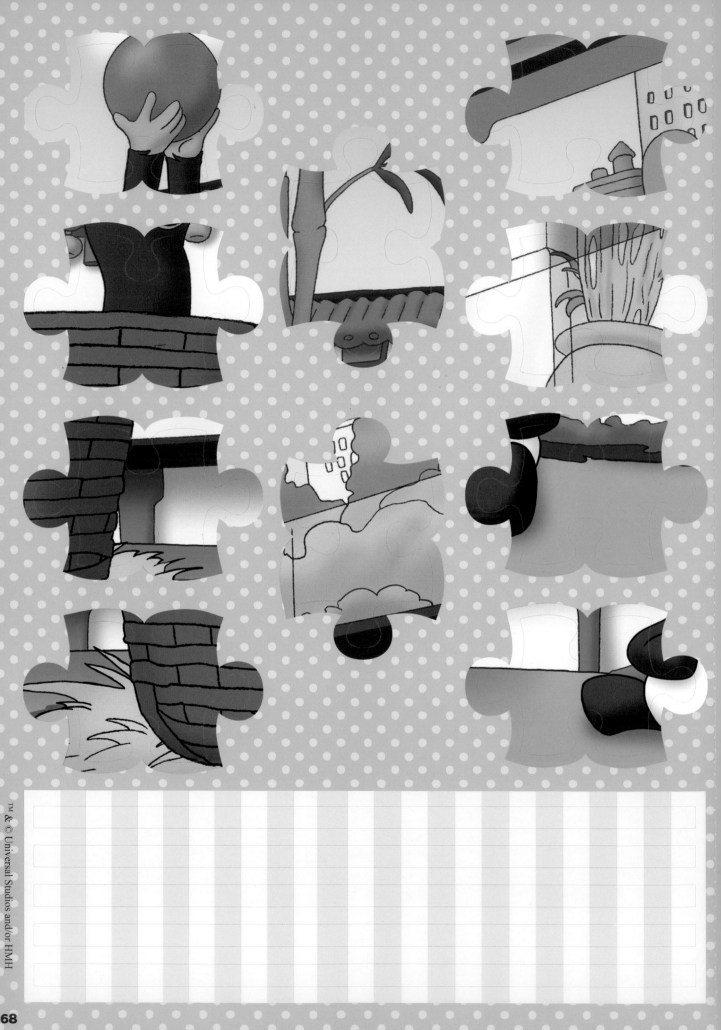

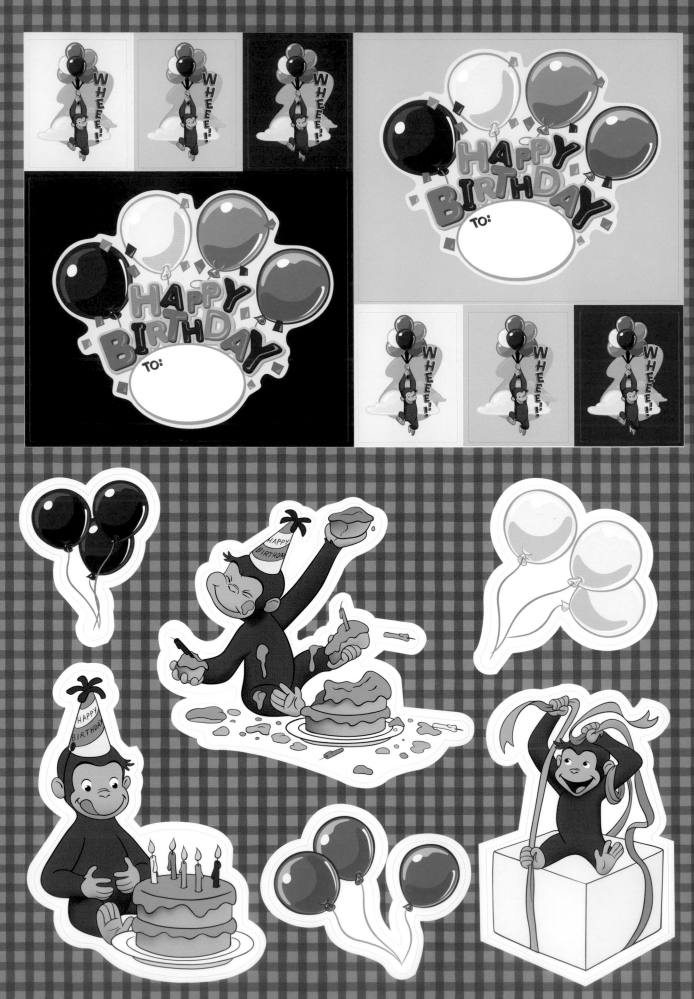

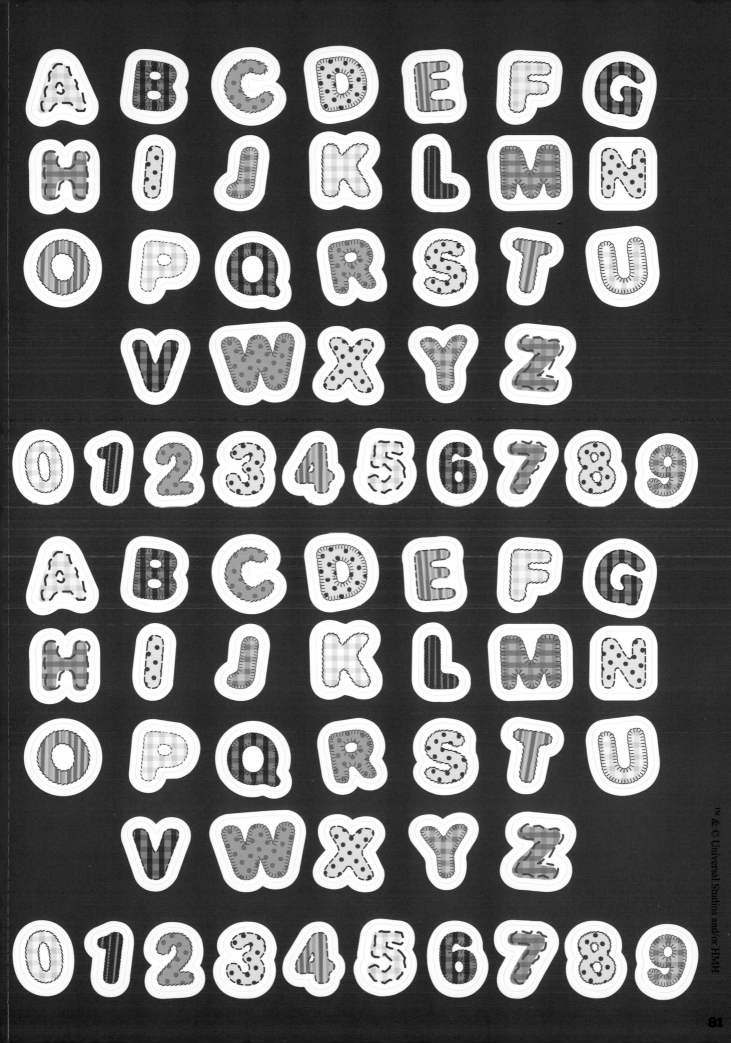

™ & © Universal Studios and/or HMH

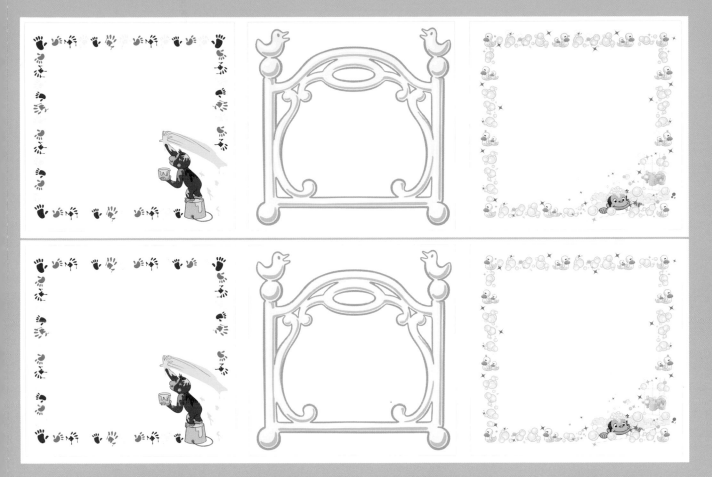

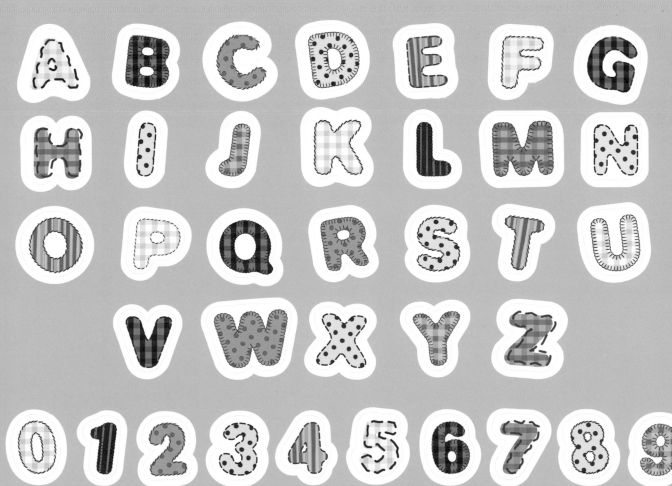

86

ABC GEORGE 123

ABC GEORGE 123

ABC GEORGE 123

ABC GEORGE 123

Color the characters using crayons or colored pencils. Then, with an adult's help, cut along the dotted lines. Insert slot A into a, B into b, etc. Stand your cut-outs and start creating your own adventures with Curious George!

f

g

F

G

With an adult's help, cut out these pictures of George and his friends. Shuffle the cards and place them all face-down on a flat surface. The first player turns two cards face-up. If they match, that player can take the pair off the board and go again. If they don't match, turn them back over, and the next player takes a turn. The player with the most matches at the end of the game is the winner.

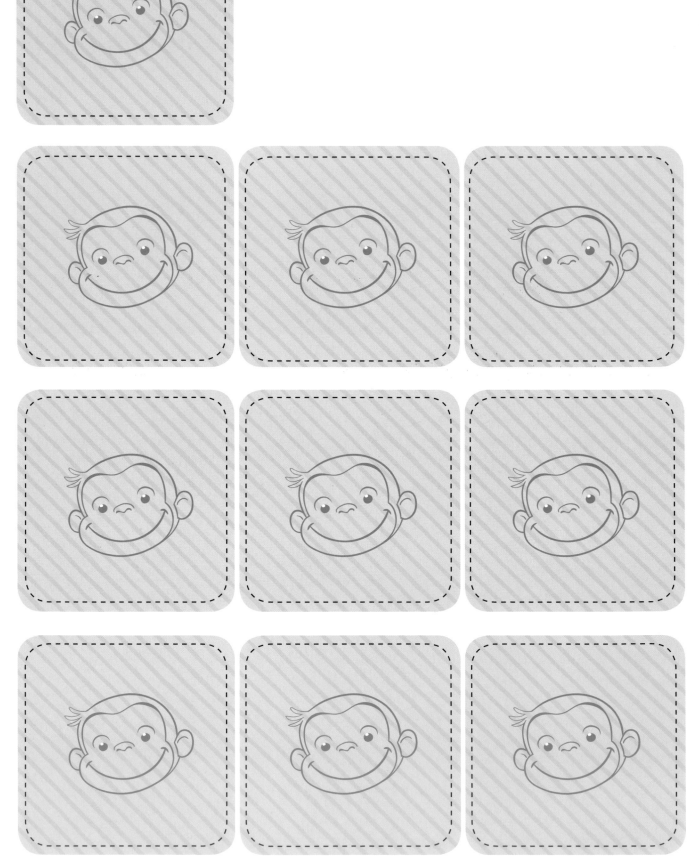

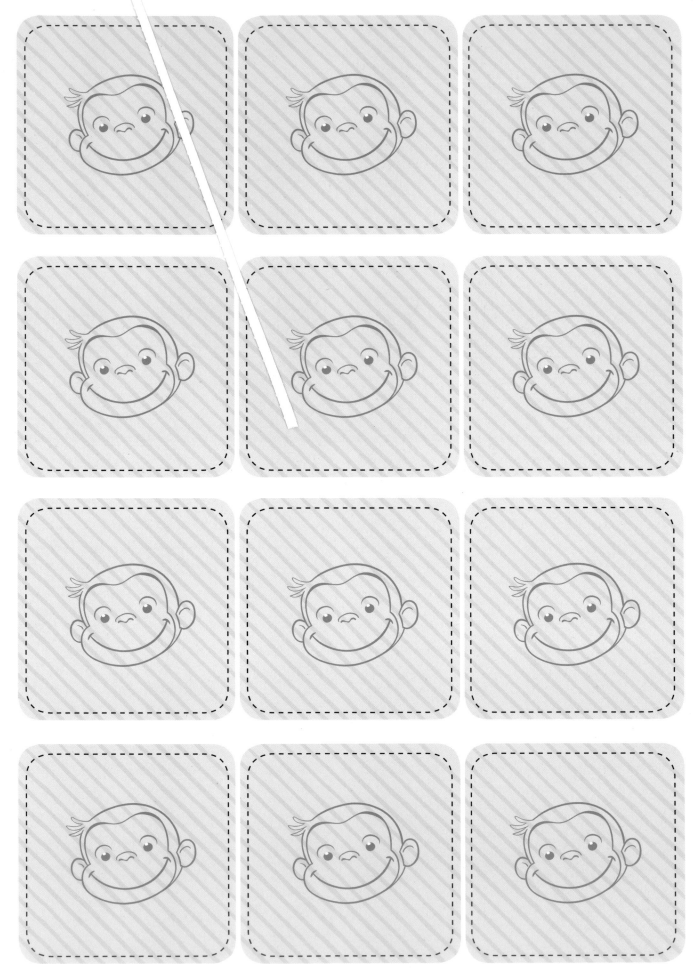